PLANET OF THE NOSE PICKERS

> YOU CAN PICK YOUR FRIENDS, AND YOU CAN PICK YOUR NOSE, BUT YOU CAN'T PICK YOUR PLANET.

Gordon Korman

Illustrated by **Victor Vaccaro**

L. A. F. :)
Books

for Children
New York

For Annabelle
MacKenzie Iserson
—G.K.

For Andrew Book—V.V.

First Edition
1 3 5 7 9 10 8 6 4 2
ISBN 0-7868-1344-X (pbk. ed.)
ISBN-7868-2571-5 (lib. ed.)

Library of Congress Cataloging-in-Publication Data on file
Korman, Gordon.
Planet of the nose pickers / by Gordon Korman ;
illustrated by Victor Vaccaro—1st ed.
p. cm.
Sequel to: Nose pickers from outer space.
Summary: Fourth grader Devin and his friend Stan, the nerdy
exchange student who is actually from the planet Pan,
try to get Earth designated as Pan's official vacation planet
so it will not get moved out past Pluto.
ISBN 0-7868-1344-X (pbk.)—ISBN 0-7868-2432-8 (lib. ed)
[1. Extraterrestrial beings—Fiction. 2. Schools—Fiction. 3. Science
fiction.] I. Vaccaro, Victor, ill. II. Title.
PZ7.K8369 Pl 2000   [Fic]—dc21
99-41922

CONTENTS

Chapter 1

MY FRIEND THE ALIEN

✳ DEVIN HUNTER'S RULES OF COOLNESS ✳

☛ **Rule 47:** When you live with an alien, you've got to be willing to make a few changes in your life.

Take me, for instance. I used to think that a nerdy little guy with a squeaky munchkin voice and thick glasses that make his eyes look like fried eggs was a dweeb. It goes to show how wrong you can be. That "dweeb" just might be a 147-year-old alien from the planet Pan, like my exchange buddy, Stan Mflxnys.

Everybody else in my fourth-grade class got to host a buddy from another part of the country. I got to host one from another part of the *galaxy*. Cody was from Texas, and Wanda was

1

from California. Those places are pretty far, sure. But Pan is eighty-five thousand light-years away. Top that.

That's a LOT OF FREQUENT FLYER MILES!

I've never been there, but I'm pretty sure it must be the most nutso place in the universe. For starters, people from Pan are called Pants. They come from the constellation of the Big Zipper. Their president is known as the Grand Pant. His assistants are the Under-Pants. I know it sounds like a comedy routine, but it's all true! I signed up for an exchange buddy, and I got Stan from Pan. My life hasn't been the same since.

I even had to change my Rules of Coolness notebook. Talk about messy! There's stuff crossed out everywhere. For example, Rule 41 started out No nose picking. I had to rewrite it to say No nose picking unless you're operating the special minicomputer that all Pants have up their schnozzes.

So when I said, "Stan, quit picking your nose!" I didn't mean that there was any actual picking going on. But there he sat, with his finger buried up to the second knuckle. And on the other side of

the den, our piano was *playing itself*! Nasal proces-sors can do that. They can do almost anything.

"Pants are not nose pickers," Stan replied, highly insulted. "I, Stan, am using my nasal processor to send ion pulses to the keys of your musical instrument."

"Well, those ion pulses are tone-deaf," I com-plained. "That's not music. It's torture."

"Really?" Stan was surprised. "That song is number one on the WPAN hit parade—'Wide Waling Chords' by the Fly Boys."

3

"It sounds like 'Old McDonald Had a Farm' mixed with a police siren," I growled. "Cut it out. I'm trying to watch TV."

"You're not watching TV," Stan accused. "You're just flipping channels. Why are we wasting time? Our social studies project is due on Friday, and we haven't even started it yet."

I shrugged. "Use your schnoz to do it." That was the best part of having Stan as an exchange buddy. With one pick of his nose, he could do the dishes, cut the grass, clean our room, or even write a ten-page essay for school, all in a split second. It was heaven. I hadn't done any homework or chores since the day the guy got here. Except for the week his nose broke down. That had almost been a total disaster.

"I'll bet your nasal processor can whip us up an A-plus social studies project," I added, through a wide, lazy yawn.

"But it can't," Stan said seriously. "The project has to be on the greatest achievements of the human race. My nasal processor can only get information about *Pan*. It knows very little Earth history."

"You mean—" I was shocked. "You mean, we're going to have to—*work*?"

The fried-egg eyes examined me closely. "Fascinating! I, Stan, have just realized something about earthling behavior. When I use my nasal processor to do all your work for you, I'm not doing you a favor."

"Yes, you are!" I howled. "A *huge* favor! Please don't stop!"

Stan shook his head. "By not working, you forget *how* to work. You become a sofa turnip."

"You mean a couch potato? No way!" But while I was saying it, I looked down at myself

lying there amidst the cushions. Candy bar wrappers and soda cans were strewn all around me. A half-eaten bag of Doritos was perched on my chest. Past it, I could just make out the beginning of my soon-to-be potbelly peeking out from the bottom of my shirt. **"Oh, no! I'm a couch potato!** I'm going to flunk social studies!"

COUCH POTATOES are MY FAVORITE VEGETABLE.

"We can't let that happen," said Stan gravely. "If either of us gets a failing grade in a school assignment, I, Stan, will have to quit the National Student Exchange Program."

That was a big problem. As nerdy as Stan was, the whole future of Earth depended on him. Stan was a travel agent, which is a really big job on Pan. Pants are the greatest tourists in the universe. They work two weeks per year, and go on vacation for the other fifty. Stan's goal was to make Earth Pan's newest vacation spot.

I held my head. "If you have to leave, you won't be able to push for Earth. So the Grand Pant will probably pick—"

"Mercury!" we chorused in agony.

Oh, no! Mercury was the other finalist for resort planet. But Earth was blocking Mercury's spectacular view of the rings of Saturn. If Mercury got picked, Earth would have to be moved—all the way out past the orbit of Pluto. **We'd freeze!**

What a mess! The decision on the new tourist planet could come any minute. Stan had his test tourists working overtime. He was sending tons of reports home to Pan about how great Earth is. How could he stop all that for something as dumb as social studies? But if we got an F on that project, he'd have to leave anyway. Either way, Earth was the big loser.

What could we do?

SOCiaL STudiEs caN bE hazardoUs tO yOur PLaNEt.

7

Chapter 2
THE UFO NUT

School was our best hope. If we could get an extension for a week or so, maybe we could save Earth by Friday, and still have the weekend to throw together a project. We had to try.

First thing in the morning, Mr. Slomin asked for progress reports on our projects. Hands shot up in our crowded classroom. Remember, we had twenty-three regular students plus fourteen exchange buddies.

Mr. Slomin picked Calista and her exchange buddy, Wanda.

"We're doing a diorama of the invention of the surfboard," announced Wanda, the Californian.

"Nice idea," the teacher approved, writing it down. "Joey and Cody, how about you?"

Cody, the visiting Texan, stood up. "Our project is about oil drilling. We're doing a diorama, too."

"Pssst!" hissed Tanner Phelps, poking me in the back. "What are you guys going to do a diorama of? The invention of nose picking?"

☞ **Rule 20:** If you don't have a good comeback, keep your mouth shut.

I gave him a dirty look, but no answer. I couldn't tell anybody that Stan wasn't really picking his nose! How would I explain what he actually *was* doing? I was the only one who knew Stan was an alien. To the rest of the kids, he was the geek in the white dress shirt and polka-dot tie. They made fun of him because he ate paper.

I'll admit it—I was the first one to point out what a weirdo Stan was. But on Pan, paper is a delicacy. They don't even have money anymore because people were snacking on their life savings. Anyway, I think it's mean to laugh at a guy because his idea of a tasty treat is *The Clearview Post*, or the paper plate instead of the sandwich. After all, everybody's different.

"Naturally, we study the *human* race because it's the only race we know," Mr. Slomin was saying. "Of course, there are many other species in the galaxy. We haven't met them yet, but we know they exist. They come in the many UFOs that visit Earth."

Everybody groaned. Mr. Slomin was a real pain in the neck about unidentified flying objects. He was even president of the Clearview UFO Society. Those guys spend every night staring into telescopes, scanning the skies for spaceships. Of course, the rest of the class was groaning because they thought Mr. Slomin was crazy. Stan and I were groaning because we knew Mr. Slomin was *right*. He had come very close to catching us one time when Stan had visitors from Pan. Even now he never looked at us without a frown of suspicion.

Mr. Slomin took note of the last few project ideas. "That's everybody except"—he consulted his list—"Devin and Stan. What are you two doing for your assignment?"

I leaped to my feet. "Oh, a diorama. Definitely."

"A diorama of what?" the teacher asked.

I was struck dumb.

"We're still working on the diorama part," Stan supplied. "When that's finished, we'll work on the 'of what' part."

Mr. Slomin glared at us. "What's that supposed to mean?"

"It means we need more time," I jumped in. "A week . . . okay, how about four days? No? Well, then, give us the extra weekend, and we'll have it ready on Monday."

Mr. Slomin slapped his desk so hard that it made a sound like a pistol shot. "No extensions," he said firmly. "I can see that you two haven't even chosen your topic!"

But later, when everyone was doing a math quiz, the teacher sidled up to us and whispered, "On second thought, I might consider giving you

the extra weekend—*if* you'll tell me what you know about the UFOs that have been sighted around Clearview lately."

"We have no idea about that," I said quickly.

He scowled. "In that case, I expect your project first thing Friday morning. **If it's one second late, you'll both receive the F's you deserve!**"

"Aw, twill!" mumbled Stan under his breath. And I knew he was really upset, because *twill* is a very bad word on Pan.

But we weren't dead yet. If we couldn't get an extension from Mr. Slomin, we had to get one from the Pan-Pan Travel Bureau.

"How do we do that?" I asked on the way home.

"It's kind of a long shot," Stan admitted. "First I, Stan, have to get approval from Agent Shkprnys on Mercury. Both travel agents must agree to the extension."

As if it wasn't bad enough that Earth was facing a trip to the deep freeze out past Pluto, Mercury's travel agent was the real kicker. Shkprnys was the greatest agent in the history of the Pan-Pan Travel Bureau. I could see Stan shaking in his boots every time he said the guy's name. Shkprnys was the agent who had the idea to open a seafood restaurant in the Crab Nebula; the Red Spot Amusement Park on Jupiter was his baby; he even spearheaded the plan to line up eighteen black holes for the best golf course in the Milky Way. The guy was a travel superstar, and a national hero on Pan.

If Earth got picked instead of Mercury, it would be the first time Shkprnys ever lost. So the odds were already stacked against us.

I opened our front door, and ushered Stan in ahead of me. "I wish there was some way I could listen in on you two guys," I said anxiously. "Remember, I'm the one whose planet is going to get frosted."

Stan looked thoughtful. "There is one possibility—" He put his finger in his nose. "Calling Agent Shkprnys. Come in, please. This is Agent Mflxnys on Earth." Then he went over to our television set, detached the cable, and shoved the end up his other nostril. Instantly, the set clicked on.

13

I WANT MY NTV:
ALL NOSE,
ALL THE TIME.

At first there was a test pattern that said PLEASE STANDETH BY. And then the picture cleared to reveal a pale, round-faced man with long hair and a small, trimmed pointy beard. Around his neck he wore a stiff white ruffle.

He said, "Forsooth, Agent Mflxnys. What dost thou want?"

I already knew who the guy really was, but it was still a shock to see him and hear the way he talked. **Shkprnys was Shakespeare—** *William Shakespeare*, the famous writer from four hundred years ago!

It was a long, crazy story. Shakespeare wasn't human; he wasn't even Shakespeare; he was an alien named Shkprnys. He lived on Earth and wrote his plays all those years ago when he was a Training Pant. But Pants can live to be a thousand. So Shakespeare—the *real* Shakespeare!—was alive and well, and working for Mercury.

"May the Crease be with you, Agent Shkprnys," said Stan respectfully. "I, Stan, have called to request a delay in the decision about the new vacation planet."

"Forsooth!" exclaimed Shakespeare, who said

that a lot. "What is thy reason for this delay?"

"It's an Earth custom," explained Stan, "known as a social studies project."

Shakespeare smiled sweetly. "Thy words have touched my heart. Thou shalt have all the time thou needest. Forsooth, I shall myself maketh the arrangements with the Pan-Pan Travel Bureau. The Grand Pant is a personal friend of mine."

Stan glowed. "Agent Shkprnys, you're as won-derful as everyone says you are. I, Stan, have never known an opponent this fair."

"We are rivals, yea, verily," replied Shkprnys smoothly. "But this is a friendly competition. May the best planet win, forsooth." The screen faded to black, and the words THE ENDE ap-peared.

Stan broke the connection by pulling the cable out of his nose.

"Seems like a pretty nice guy," I commented. "Are you sure we can trust him?"

Stan was offended. "*Trust* him?! Devin, that's Shkprnys the One and Only! He wrote the words 'To thine own self be true'! What could be more honest than that?"

"Just checking," I said soothingly.

☞ **Rule 37:** Never insult another guy's hero.

Chapter 3

WHO CRASHED THE
FLYING SAUCER?

That night I enjoyed the first decent sleep I'd had in days. Earth wasn't exactly safe yet. But at least I knew we weren't going to wake up frozen in a block of ice out past Pluto, where the sun looks as bright as a ten-watt bulb. Good old Shakespeare. He was starting to be my hero, too.

I'M TOUCHED.

Stan and I had even gotten started on our social studies project. My dad had given us a big wooden crate, and we'd painted it and everything. It was drying overnight in the backyard. All we had to do was figure out what to stick in it. We wouldn't get an A-plus, but at least we wouldn't flunk.

So we were sleeping away—I'd finally learned to tune out Stan's snoring. (Because of his nose computer, he made a noise like the hum of a microwave oven.) Then, all of a sudden,

CRASH!!!

Instantly awake and alert, we both jumped up and ran to the window. There was our diorama box, busted into a million pieces. And those million pieces were on fire. Above the flames, like a frying pan on a gas stove, was perched a spaceship.

I glared at Stan.

He looked sheepish. "It's one of ours. A Button-Fly 501 Space Cruiser."

I knew that already. I'd seen a ship from Pan. I recognized the shape—shallow and eight-sided, like a giant stop sign. The door started as a tiny dot, then grew and grew. A staircase descended, and a red carpet unrolled across the lawn.

Out stepped two Pants I had seen before. They were dressed exactly like Stan, with the same white dress shirts, and black polka-dot ties that were on so tight they stuck out in front. Their names were Zgrbnys the Extremely Wise and Gthrmnys the Utterly Clever. They were members of the most respected class on Pan—professional thinkers known as the Smarty-Pants.

It's pretty hard for us earthlings to get a sense of just how intelligent these guys have to be. Compared to them, **Einstein was a hamster.** The Smarty-Pants can think in six dimensions. Their IQs are so large that even they can't count that high. They can read the entire dictionary in five minutes, and remember most of the words.

They know the secret of happiness, the infinity times table, and even why manhole covers are round. It's unbelievably hard to become a Smarty-Pant. Stan used to be in Smarty-Pants University, but he got kicked out because he flubbed the question about the manhole covers.

Careful not to wake up my family, Stan and I crept downstairs and let ourselves out into the yard. I kind of hung back, but Stan stepped forward for the formal greeting.

"Welcome, Zgrbnys and Gthrmnys. May the Crease be with you."

Zgrbnys looked disgusted. "The Crease should have been with Gthrmnys when he was piloting through the Great Magellanic Cloud! **My nine-hundred-year-old grandmother flies better than that!**"

Gthrmnys flushed bright red. "The sun got in my eyes!"

"The sun was forty light-years away!" snapped Zgrbnys. "We were in the blackness of space!"

"The black got in my eyes!" Gthrmnys insisted.

"What happened?" Stan asked anxiously.

"We sideswiped an asteroid," said Zgrbnys sourly. "It was all his fault."

"Was not!"

"Was so!"

INTErSTELLar road ragE.

Stan regarded the small dent in the silver side of the craft. "That doesn't look too bad. Your nasal processors could fix it in no time."

"But what about the scratch?" demanded Zgrbnys furiously. "Nasal processors can fix a dent, but they can't match paint!"

"If we go back to Pan with a scratch on our ship," complained Gthrmnys, "people might think we did something—dumb!"

Stan was horrified. "No one could ever think that about a Smarty-Pant!"

I stepped forward. "Why don't you go to Larson's Hardware Store?"

Zgrbnys looked at me like I was a very pesky insect. "Quiet, earthling. Your primitive brain cannot begin to understand our situation."

I shrugged. "What's to understand? You had an accident, and now you're too embarrassed to own up. That's why you need Larson's. They're great at matching paint."

"This earthling is wise," observed Gthrmnys.

Stan introduced me. "This is my friend Devin Hunter. You won't meet a smarter earthling. He wrote the Rules of Coolness that I put in my last report."

"Yes, I read these rules," sneered Zgrbnys. "They are wrong. They would have no effect whatsoever on the temperature, which, I should point out, is cool enough."

I took my exchange buddy aside. "Listen,

Stan, are you sure these guys are real Smarty-Pants? They don't seem that bright to me."

But Stan's fried-egg eyes were practically whirling with excitement. "Don't you see, Devin? This is a big chance for us! If we can help Zgrbnys and Gthrmnys with their problem, they'll put in a good word for Earth with the Grand Pant!"

"But how do we pull that off?" I demanded. "My folks are going to notice a spaceship standing in the backyard, you know! Not to mention two six-foot dweebs arguing about who crashed the flying saucer! We'll never come up with a cover story for all that!"

Stan looked at me like I was crazy. "Devin, we have two of the greatest minds in the galaxy here to help us." He turned to the Smarty-Pants. "Please use your natural super-genius to devise a believable story for Devin's family."

"Nothing could be simpler," said Zgrbnys smugly. "We'll say that the ship is a giant silver octagonal mushroom that has sprung up out of the ground overnight."

Of course! Why didn't I think of that?

"And we," added Gthrmnys with enthusiasm, "are inspectors from the *Guinness Book of World Records*, in charge of their mushroom department."

I looked at Stan, but he was completely convinced. I guess when you live 147 years hearing about how brilliant Smarty-Pants are, it's pretty hard to believe that they could be a couple of knuckleheads like this pair.

"All right," I said. "Here's what we're going to do. . . ."

Chapter 4

UNCLE ZACK AND UNCLE GUS

When I heard the scream, I knew Mom had discovered the Smarty-Pants in the guest room.

I leaped out of bed and went tearing down the hall. "Don't worry, Mom!"

She was pointing at the doorway. "But there are two strange men in there!"

"They're not strange," I assured her. **"Well, okay, maybe they're a little strange.** But they're Stan's uncles. They pulled an all-nighter on the bus from—Chicago. I didn't want to wake you, so I set them up in the guest room."

She looked only slightly relieved. "Oh. They're—quite welcome, of course. Uh—just how long are they planning to stay?"

"Only a couple of days," I assured her. "They're helping us with our social studies project. It's a big surprise, so could you please tell Lindsay and Roscoe and Dad to stay away from the garage?"

That's where we'd hidden the spaceship. And just in case someone peeked in the window, we had it draped with a New York Yankees tarpaulin that Zgrbnys and Gthrmnys happened to have in the cargo bay.

I sweated all through breakfast. The whole family was there, meeting Uncle Zack and Uncle Gus. I mean, we couldn't very well call them by their real names, could we?

Wouldn't you know it—those so-called geniuses couldn't remember which one was supposed to be Zack, and which one was supposed to be Gus.

"So," said my father, pouring out more coffee, "what do you fellows do for a living?"

"They're in the intelligence business," supplied Stan.

"They're *spies*?" blurted my older brother, Roscoe.

"Of course not," said Zgrbnys. "We're geniuses."

Mom smiled. "But what actual job do you do?"

"Thinking, mostly," put in Gthrmnys. "But there's also a lot of pondering, ruminating, cogitating, and envisioning."

AND dictioNary swaLLOWINg.

"We sometimes put in two-hour days," added Zgrbnys.

"Oh," nodded Dad. "Consultants."

Roscoe stared at the sports section of the morning paper. "Hey, this is weird. Someone stole the giant tarp that covers the infield at Yankee Stadium. And get this—the groundskeeper insists he saw a UFO fly away with it."

"I wonder what happened to it," mused Mom.

"Well, it's not in the garage, that's for sure," announced Gthrmnys.

I choked. Orange juice really stings when you snort it out your nose.

Gthrmnys popped his napkin into his mouth and chewed happily. Then he stuck his hand in the maple syrup, came up with a gooey, dripping glob, and washed his face with it.

"Ooooh!" exclaimed my kid sister, Lindsay.

27

"That's **g r o s s !** "

But Dad was laughing. "Gus, you're a riot! You really know how to entertain the kids."

"Thank you," chorused both Smarty-Pants.

Gthrmnys got annoyed. "I'm Gus!"

"No, *I'm* Gus!"

Fungus, our cocker spaniel, jumped up onto the table, and started to lick "Uncle Gus's" sweet sticky face. Fungus barked.

Gthrmnys barked back.

Lindsay clapped her hands with delight. "You talk to dogs, too, just like Stan!"

I held my head. I'd forgotten that the nasal processors have Pan-Tran translators that can speak Dog. Oh, man, it just couldn't get any worse than this!

The doorbell rang. Mom went to answer it.

"Oh, hello, Mr. Slomin. What brings you here so early in the morning? Do you need to speak with Devin and Stan?"

I knew Mr. Slomin was there in the kitchen without even turning around. I could feel his eyes burning into the back of my neck.

"I'm not here as a teacher," Mr. Slomin said sternly. "This is official business of the UFO Society. One of our members spotted a space-craft landing in this area last night. Did anyone here notice anything?"

"We were all asleep," said my father. "Maybe Stan's uncles saw something. They got in pretty late."

"Our specialty is thinking, not observing," put in Gthrmnys.

29

"Uncles?" Mr. Slomin looked closely at Zgrbnys and Gthrmnys. "Yes, I see the family resemblance. Well, Mr. and Mrs. Hunter, I'll get to the point. There is something very suspicious in your garage. It's covered by a New York Yankees tarpaulin—exactly the kind that was stolen by a UFO last night. Please unlock the garage at once."

"Oh," chuckled my dad. "You're talking about the boys' social studies project. They're very excited about it. We all promised to stay away so as not to spoil their surprise."

"The mushroom story would have been much more believable," Zgrbnys muttered to Stan.

I had a sickening feeling that school was going to be torture today.

Sure enough, Mr. Slomin was like a bloodhound. He kept saying things like, "You boys look pretty tired. Were you up in the middle of the night, maybe?" and "Where would you get a Yankees tarpaulin? They don't sell them in stores."

"This is agony!" I whispered to Stan at recess.

Stan nodded. "We were fortunate that your parents wouldn't let him in the garage."

I groaned. "You know what the worst part is? Those two so-called geniuses are all alone in our house! Who knows what kind of trouble they're getting into right now?"

Stan was horrified. "Devin, how can you say that? They're *Smarty-Pants*! They know why manhole covers are round! Whatever they do, I, Stan, am sure it will be exactly the right thing!"

I practically shook all the way home. I'm not sure what I expected to see—maybe a pile of rubble where our house once stood. And two interstellar dweebs with their fingers up their noses, telling me it was really a mushroom that looked exactly like a busted-up house!

We came to our block and rounded the corner. The house was still there, thank goodness. But Zgrbnys and Gthrmnys were nowhere to be found.

Chapter 5

NOSE PICKERS ON TV

"Oh, no!" I moaned. "Those two idiots are on the loose in Clearview!"

"Devin!" Stan was really angry with me. "What's the matter with you? They're not 'on the loose.' They used their super-intelligence to decide exactly the best place to be, and they went there."

We checked the garage. Under the tarp, the spaceship was completely repaired, including the touch-up paint.

"They're ready to go!" I wailed. **"Why aren't they gone?"**

"Have a little faith," Stan scolded me. "They know best. Knowing is their business. Look at Fungus. He isn't worried."

That's because Fungus is a *dog*. If he has a

bowl of kibble, and the toilet seat is up, what does he have to worry about?

Lindsay came home. Roscoe came home. Mom and Dad came home. No Smarty-Pants.

"Where are Zack and Gus?" asked Dad, stowing his briefcase.

"Out," I said faintly.

My mom started rattling around in the kitchen. "Should we hold supper for them?"

Stan leaned over to my ear and whispered, "The Sears catalog is unharmed, but the Yellow Pages are chewed through to the L's."

"I think they ate already," I called to Mom.

By seven o'clock, I was really starting to panic. I know Rule 3 says Never panic. But I was ready to phone all the jails to see if the cops had arrested any nose pickers.

Never fingerprint a nose picker.

"Devin! Stan! Come quick!" called my mother from the den. "*Jeopardy!*'s on."

"Not now," I yelled back.

"But the show is on tour this week. Tonight they're broadcasting from *Clearview*! We can't miss it."

34

So we joined the rest of the family in the den. It's not often that a dinky town like Clearview gets to host a big-time TV show like *Jeopardy!* When we got there, Alex Trebek was introducing the evening's contestants.

"Please welcome a retired schoolteacher from Hicksville, New York, Miss Zelda Gluck. And two consultants, both from Pan, Illinois, Gus Gthrmnys and Zack Zgrbnys."

I wheezed so hard that I must have sucked in half the air in the room. Our two Smarty-Pants were standing right there with Alex Trebek on national TV!

IS ALEX TREbEK aN aLiEN, tOO? NO, JUST a CaNadiaN.

"Stan, look!" exclaimed Roscoe. "It's your uncles! Why didn't they tell us they were going to be on *Jeopardy!*?"

Because they *weren't* going to be on *Jeopardy!* Not until they used their nose computers, I'll bet, to get on the contestant list!

Stan was practically glowing. "Devin!" he whispered. "This is the best possible thing that could have happened!"

"Just peachy!" I groaned sarcastically.

"No, really," he insisted. "If the Smarty-Pants have a good time here on Earth, they'll pass that along in their report to the Grand Pant. And what could be more fun for Smarty-Pants than showing off how smart they are?"

"They've already shown *us* how smart they are," I murmured tragically.

"Yes, but now they'll get to show an entire planet!"

"Hey, look, Stan," piped up Lindsay. *"Your uncles are picking their noses on TV!"*

I couldn't take it another second. "We've got to get down to that studio!"

We raced out. I jumped on my bike and hauled Stan up onto the handlebars. Then I pedaled like mad for downtown and the TV studio that was broadcasting *Jeopardy!*

The place was packed, but Stan used his nasal processor to get us front row seats.

The show was almost over. And I have to say that the "uncles" were doing really well. They were tied with 38,700 dollars each. Miss Gluck was in third place with three dollars.

"Wow!" I whispered to Stan. "I've never seen anybody run up so much money on *Jeopardy!* before."

He was smug. "There's never been any Smarty-Pants on *Jeopardy!* before."

"Well, this is the most exciting duel we've had in a long time!" enthused Alex Trebek. "Gus and Zack have not made a single mistake between them. That's something to bear in mind as our contestants think of their secret wagers for Final Jeopardy!"

"I don't have to make a secret wager," announced Gthrmnys. "I will, of course, bet everything."

"I, too, bet everything," said Gthrmnys stoutly.

The studio audience gave them a big cheer.

The two Smarty-Pants stuck their fingers in their noses in intense concentration.

The category was Trivia. Alex Trebek read out the final answer. The three contestants had to come up with the question.

"'This is the reason manhole covers are round.'"

I thought Stan was going to launch himself up through the ceiling of the studio. "They know this!" he chortled gleefully. "All Smarty-Pants know this! It's the number one fact at Smarty-Pants University!"

"So how come they're not writing?" I asked.

It was true. Zgrbnys and Gthrmnys stood frozen with their fingers up their noses. They looked like a couple of nose-picking statues. The music played; the time ran out.

Miss Gluck had no answer.

"What was your wager?" asked Alex Trebek. "Ah, two dollars. That leaves you with a total of one dollar. Now we move on to the two gentlemen from Illinois. Will this be a tiebreaker? Will it be the biggest payoff in *Jeopardy!* history? Let's see what you've written."

The screens in front of Zgrbnys and Gthrmnys lit up. They were both blank.

Stan was thunderstruck. "But they *know* this!"

Alex Trebek looked grave. "Oooh, I'm sorry, fellows. Since you bet everything, your winnings are reset to zero. Miss Gluck, you are our new *Jeopardy!* champion, with a grand total of one dollar! Congratulations!"

The audience didn't clap. They didn't even move. No one had ever seen so much money wiped out in the wink of an eye.

"But why didn't they answer?" Stan barely whispered.

The last thing that was broadcast on TV was Zgrbnys and Gthrmnys trying to strangle each other.

Then the network cut to a commercial.

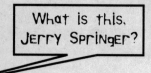

What is this, Jerry Springer?

Chapter 6

ALL ABOARD FOR OUTER SPACE

It's a good thing Stan and I were there to help Alex Trebek break up the fight. What a great guy! Brave, too. He didn't even complain when Zgrbnys gave him a fat lip. He said it didn't hurt much, and makeup could take care of it for tomorrow's show. Then he bundled all four of us, and my bike, into a *Jeopardy!* van, and had us driven home.

Out on the front porch, Stan turned his fried-egg eyes on his fellow Pants. "I, Stan, know why you didn't answer that last question."

Zgrbnys looked embarrassed. "You do?"

Stan nodded. "Manhole covers are classified information, right? You can't give the secret away to non-Smarty-Pants!"

I laughed in all three of their faces. "I've flunked enough tests to be able to recognize someone who doesn't have a clue what the answer is. And when Alex Trebek asked about manhole covers, you two were as blank as a TV screen with the cable out. You guys have *no idea* why manhole covers are round, do you?"

Zgrbnys turned on Gthrmnys. "Why didn't you tell me you didn't know?"

"Why didn't *you* tell me *you* didn't know?"

"But didn't you have to know it to pass the

Smarty-Pants Aptitude Test?" asked Stan.

"It wasn't on the test," Zgrbnys admitted, shamefaced.

"No one ever asked me, either," confirmed Gthrmnys, with a heavy sigh. "And now we'll be kicked out of the Smarty-Pants Union."

That gave me an idea. "Who's going to know except me and Stan? We'll make you a deal. We won't tell anybody about the manhole covers thing if you promise to put in a *very* good word for Earth to the Grand Pant."

They looked bewildered. "What for?"

"So we'll get picked for vacation planet," I explained, exasperated. "The big decision is coming up, you know."

"But that decision has already been made," said Zgrbnys. **"Earth lost."**

"Not possible!" gasped Stan. "I, Stan, made an agreement with Agent Shkprnys on Mercury—"

"Agent Shkprnys isn't on Mercury," said Gthrmnys. "He's been back on Pan for days, shaking hands and kissing babies. He told the Pan-Pan Travel Bureau that you quit, and that's why the reports stopped coming."

"Twill!" cried Stan. "Shkprnys tricked us!"

"Watch your language!" snapped Zgrbnys. "You don't say the 'T' word in front of Smarty-Pants!"

I admit it; I went nuts. "Oh, no! It's really happening! We're going out past Pluto! And I wouldn't let Mom buy me any long johns because they broke ☛ **Rule 43: Long johns look like thermal ballet tights!** It's over! It's over—"

"Not yet," Stan interrupted grimly. "I, Stan, am going to Pan to tell Earth's side of the story. And you, Devin, are coming with me."

I stared at him. "Are you nuts? Dad wouldn't even sign the permission slip for the overnight at Scout camp! You think he's not going to notice if I travel to another planet eighty-five thousand light-years away?"

Zgrbnys butted in. "Your limited intelligence cannot understand space travel. It takes only a few hours to fly to Pan. But here on Earth, sixty years go by."

"Sixty years?!" I howled.

"But coming home," Gthrmnys took up the explanation, "you *lose* sixty years, and arrive

only a few seconds after you left. Your family will never know you have been gone. See how simple it is?"

My head was spinning. Okay, I was going to Pan. I had no choice. I owed that much to my family and my fellow earthlings.

Please, please, *please* let Earth be here when I get back!

> MaKe sure you return your library books before you go.

Chapter 7

A FLOATING MUSHROOM

"All right, I'll go," I announced. "But we've got to figure out a way to get the spaceship out of the garage and take off without my parents noticing."

Stan shrugged. "That should be no problem at all. We've got two of the keenest minds in the galaxy to help us out."

"Of course!" exclaimed Zgrbnys. "We will re-program our nasal processors to fill your house with several thousand crickets. They will chirp so loudly that it will cover up the sound of the spaceship."

That didn't sound too good to me. "And how do we get rid of the crickets afterward?"

Gthrmnys dismissed this with a wave of his

> That kind of plan really bugs people.

hand. "Since we will be gone, that will be your family's problem."

"No crickets," I said firmly. "Stan and I are going to go in there and play the TV loud. Just beep Stan's nose computer when you've got the ship ready. I'll get you the garage door opener." I ran to the car, which was parked on the street. I snatched the clip-on remote control from the sun shade and handed it to Zgrbnys.

"I will need several hours to analyze this high technology," the Smarty-Pant told me.

I was disgusted. "There's only one button! Even you guys couldn't mess it up!"

Then came the toughest job of the night—walking into the den like everything was normal.

"Stan," said my mother, "are your uncles all right? We saw what happened on *Jeopardy!*"

"Oh, they're fine, Mrs. Hunter."

"Did they kill each other?" piped up Lindsay.

Through the window I could see the garage door opening. I leaned over and bumped up the TV volume a couple of notches.

"Devin, that's a little loud," my father complained.

"Sorry, Dad, can't hear you." I raised the sound even higher.

Roscoe jumped in. "How come Devin's allowed to blast the TV, but I get in trouble if I turn up my stereo?"

I caught a brief glimpse of the spaceship backing out of the garage, hovering a foot above the driveway. I punched the volume up to maximum.

"Devin!" screeched my mother. "Have you lost your mind?"

I looked at Stan, but he shook his head. No signal yet from the Smarty-Pants.

And then, over the blaring of the TV, I could just make out an all-too-familiar voice:

"Stop in the name of planetary defense!"

GUESS whO?

My heart leaped up into my throat. It was Mr. Slomin! And this time he had a bona fide UFO in his sights!

"I—I—I gotta check the twist-ties on the garbage!" I grabbed Stan, and we bolted out of the house like we'd been shot from a cannon.

Outside, a horrifying sight met my eyes. The ship hung there, its round door open wide.

Gthrmnys was halfway up the staircase, caught in the beam of Mr. Slomin's flashlight.

"Back away from that spacecraft!" bellowed our teacher.

Gthrmnys tossed him a haughty look. "What spacecraft?"

It was stupid, but you had to admire the guy's nerve.

"It's not a ship!" called Zgrbnys from inside. "It's a large floating mushroom—"

Before he could finish, things got a little wild. Gthrmnys tried to make it into the ship, but Mr. Slomin ran up, grabbed him by the foot, and hung on.

"Let me go, you primitive life-form!" cried Gthrmnys.

With a wild bark, Fungus erupted out of his doghouse, and fastened his teeth on Mr. Slomin's ankle.

"Yeow!"

The teacher let go, and Gthrmnys rushed aboard.

Stan squeezed my arm. "Devin—the door!"

I looked. The black circle was growing smaller. "Run!" I bellowed.

Stan raced up the stairs and hurled himself inside. "Hurry!" he urged me.

I was hot on his heels, screaming all the way. I felt the carpet and stairway start to fold up under me. I launched myself like a torpedo through the rapidly shrinking door. *Wham!* I hit the floor of the cabin hard, and scrambled back to my feet. "Safe!" I cried, weak with relief.

And then, a split second before the opening spiraled shut, Mr. Slomin squeezed through. Fungus was still clamped heroically onto his leg. The door became a dot, and then winked out of existence.

"Stop!" I hollered. "Our teacher's on board!"

But by the time the words were out of my mouth, our house was a tiny speck, and we were higher up than I'd ever been before, even on an airplane.

That's when I noticed the garage door opener clipped to Gthrmnys's shirt pocket. I snatched it away and snapped it onto my belt. I had to get this back to Mom and Dad.

But first it was going to take a little ride. We all were.

Chapter 8

ALIEN ABDUCTION

"*Alien abduction!*" bellowed Mr. Slomin. "*Alien abduction! HELP!*"

"You haven't been abducted, earthling," called Zgrbnys from the controls. "You jumped on board."

Mr. Slomin turned blazing eyes on Stan. "I was right! There *have* been UFOs in Clearview! And *you* have been cooperating with the aliens!"

"Incorrect, Mr. Slomin," Stan explained. "I, Stan, *am* an alien. I am Agent Mflxnys of the Pan-Pan Travel Bureau, under command of His Most Tailored Majesty, the Grand Pant."

The teacher turned to me. "How could *you* go along with all this, Devin? Don't you have any loyalty to your planet?"

He'd show you his business card, but he ate it.

I was so upset that I couldn't even get my mouth to work. Here I was, a kid who'd never even been to sleepaway camp, heading for the other side of the galaxy just to save Earth. And my own teacher was calling me a traitor!

"It's not what you think—" I began.

But Mr. Slomin had shifted his attention to the Smarty-Pants at the controls.

"As President of the UFO Society, it is my duty to warn you that you're making a big mistake! We may not have fancy ships like this, but **when it comes to kicking butt, Earth is the best there is!** If you don't take me back this minute and surrender yourselves to our authorities, Earth is going to send a fleet to wipe up the galaxy with you guys!"

Zgrbnys and Gthrmnys started laughing so hard I was afraid they were going to crash the ship.

"Oh!" Zgrbnys gasped. "That's rich! That Pan might have something to fear from a Q-class planet like Earth!"

"And their fleet!" giggled Gthrmnys. "Why, the fastest rocket on Earth would take over a

billion years to get halfway to Pan! Ooooh, we're so scared!"

I thought Mr. Slomin was going to blow a gasket. "Who are you calling Q-class? Class A, all the way! That's our motto! Earth is no pushover! We have *nuclear power*!"

That made the Smarty-Pants laugh harder. And even Stan, who had much better manners, couldn't hold back a chuckle or two.

"I'm so sorry," he apologized. "I, Stan, don't mean to be rude. **But on Pan, we use nuclear power for our popcorn poppers and toilet flushers.** Our main source of energy is the Crease."

The Crease is a wrinkle in the fabric of space, whatever that means. Stan says there's unlimited energy coming from it. Yeah, I know, he could be making it up. But you kind of had to believe it. There we were, after all, streaking across the sky.

Suddenly, the ship dipped and swerved, knocking us all off our feet. I fell into Stan, and the two of us tripped over Fungus. Mr. Slomin's feet slipped out from under him, and he landed flat on his back and whacked his head on the shiny silver floor. He lay there, out cold and snoring.

"It might get a little bumpy back there as we land," came a very late warning from pilot Zgrbnys.

I was amazed. "Are we at Pan already?"

"No," said Gthrmnys. "St. Louis."

"*St. Louis!?*" Maybe the Crease wasn't such hot stuff after all.

"We have to pick up another passenger," Stan explained. "One of my test tourists needs a ride home." The test tourists were Pants like Stan. They posed as humans while doing vacation research on Earth.

I looked away from the window because it was making me dizzy. One second, we were miles above Earth. The next, we were touching down in a dark backyard somewhere in St. Louis, Missouri.

The door opened, and the staircase and red carpet descended.

"Welcome, Mgwrnys the Swinger," Stan greeted his employee.

I gawked. Standing right in the doorway was none other than Mark McGwire of the St. Louis Cardinals, the home run king!

"Stan!" I gasped. "Mark McGwire is an alien?"

Stan shrugged. "You didn't think a mere earthling could hit like that, did you?"

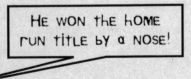

HE WON THE HOME RUN TITLE BY a NOSE!

Chapter 9

LEFT TURN AT THE GLOBULAR CLUSTER

Zoom! We were off again. I could tell that this time we were going a lot farther than St. Louis. When I looked back out the window, Earth was just a tiny blue marble against a starry sky that stretched on forever.

Suddenly, I felt a lump in my throat the size of an apple. Sure, I knew I was breaking ☛ **Rule 12: Homesickness is for losers.** But my whole family was back on Earth, and everybody I knew. If something went wrong on this trip, I would never see them again. Mom, Dad, Lindsay, Roscoe—well, to be honest, half a galaxy seemed like a pretty good barrier between Roscoe and me. But he *was* my brother, and I would probably miss him.

> DOES ANYONE HEAR VIOLIN MUSIC?

Stan must have noticed my long face. He came and sat down beside me, placing a comforting hand on my shoulder. "Don't worry, Devin. I know eighty-five thousand light-years seems like a long way. But for us at the Pan-Pan Travel Bureau, it's like a Weekend Getaway Special. I, Stan, know Pants who'll journey forty thousand light-years just to have dinner at a restaurant with really good napkins. You're thinking about this like an earthling. Try to take the Pant view."

I brightened a little. If there was one good thing to come from this terrible mess, with Earth being in such danger and all, it was my friendship with Stan Mflxnys. He wasn't cool; but as dweebs went, he was the best.

Near the cargo hatch, Fungus and Mark McGwire were deep in conversation. It sounded like the dog pound back there. You never heard so much barking.

I nudged Stan. "What are they talking about?"

"Oh," Stan said airily. "Fungus noticed a little kink in Mgwrnys's swing last season. He's giving him a few pointers."

I goggled. My dog, who begs for table scraps and drinks out of the toilet, was coaching the great Mark McGwire! What a galaxy!

"Hey, Stan," I whispered. "Are you sure those two Smarty-Pants are safe enough drivers? They're staring at their ties instead of, you know, the road."

Stan looked surprised. "Of course they are. How can a pilot navigate without his tie?"

I was mystified. "Polka dots tell you where to go?"

"They're not polka dots," he explained. "They're star maps. We Pants can find our way home from anywhere. Of course, when you enter a new sector, you have to change ties."

According to the ties, our flight plan took us out of the solar system, past the Big Dipper, with a left turn at Globular Cluster M11, and straight on to the red giant star, Ama.

"And that's close to Pan?" I asked.

"Oh, no," Stan said seriously. "In fact, Ama is even farther from Pan than Earth."

I was confused. "You mean we're flying in the wrong direction?"

Stan shook his head. "You see, Ama is right next to the entrance to hyperspace. In hyperspace, we can pick up a shortcut all the way to Pan on the other side of the galaxy. We Pants call it the Pan-Ama Canal."

Our spaceship gave a sickening lurch.

I nearly jumped out of my skin. "What was that?"

Pilot Zgrbnys had the answer. "Hyperspace! Tighten your suspenders and hang on to your belt loops!"

"That's an old saying on Pan," Stan whispered to me.

Hyperspace was kind of scary. There are no stars, so it's completely black in there, except for your own running lights. And you're moving so fast you can hear it. It sounds like "Flight of the Bumblebee" at a hundred times normal speed, being played by a mosquito on a tiny kazoo. We were vibrating so much that Fungus started to howl, and Mr. Slomin woke up. And then, suddenly, it all stopped, and we were out.

I ran to the window. There it was—the constellation of the Big Zipper. It really *was* a zipper—hundreds of stars lined up in pairs. And at the very top—

"Devin, look!" cried Stan joyfully. "It's Pan!"

"Well, we made it," declared Zgrbnys as we began to descend. "A brilliant job of piloting by me."

"You never could have done it without my expert navigation," put in Gthrmnys.

"Big deal!" snorted his partner. **"You can read a tie."**

As we broke through the clouds, I could

see that the land was kind of a khaki color.

"This region is called the Panhandle," my exchange buddy explained. "I, Stan, grew up here."

We set down with a soft bump. A recorded voice announced, *"Welcome to Pan Intergalactic Spaceport, located in the beautiful twin cities of Levi-Strauss. This greeting is brought to you by the planet Mercury—Pan's newest resort, a barren, scorched wasteland, handpicked by Agent Shkprnys himself. Leave your coat at home, and bring your gas mask, because the air on Mercury is one-hundred-percent poisonous. Gaze up at the breathtaking rings of Saturn, with no other planet blocking your perfect view. Remember: to tan or not to tan—that is the question on Mercury."*

I turned horrified eyes to Stan. "You mean they've moved Earth *already*?"

"It's just a commercial," Stan soothed. "Shkprnys is famous for advertising a place before it opens. We still have time to reach the Grand Pant. Okay, take off your shoes."

"Why?" I asked.

Stan looked at me like I had a cabbage for a

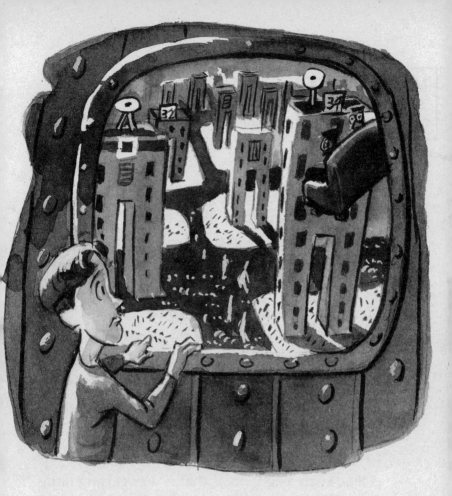

head. "You don't want to track dirt on the carpet, do you?"

I frowned. "What carpet? We're *outside*."

"Outside is where the carpet is," Stan explained.

I peered through the window. That khaki

My mom did the same thing with our living room.

color—it was fuzzy shag carpeting!

"You mean you've carpeted—"

"The whole planet," finished Stan.

"What for?"

"It's a long story," Stan admitted. "A few hundred years ago, the Smarty-Pants were experimenting with a combination intelligence booster and root beer. They constructed the galaxy's first trillion-gallon soda-pop can. Wouldn't you know it? There was an earthquake, and the can got shaken up."

I clued in. "Don't tell me they opened it."

He nodded sadly. "It sprayed the whole planet. Even today, the polar ice caps are covered in frozen root beer. And when the grass started dying, the Grand Pant had no choice but to carpet everything. But the Designer Jeans picked such a light color that it was getting filthy all the time. Do you know how much it costs to steam-clean three hundred billion square feet of carpet?"

"I guess a lot."

"Over fifty million Pantaloons," Stan informed me. "And that's with a coupon. The Pocket, our planetary treasury, was going broke. The Grand Pant had to outlaw shoes to avoid a depression."

I stepped out of my sneakers and kicked them under my chair. A whole planet where shoes are illegal, thanks to the genius Smarty-Pants. Didn't it figure?

Outside the ship, Stan stuck his nose in a slot marked INSPECTION STATION—SNORT HERE. I had to register my garage door opener as an alien device. Fungus had to do the same with his dog collar. So did Mark McGwire with his baseball bat.

"Where's Mr. Slomin?" I asked Stan.

Before he could answer, a booming voice thundered, "You people will rue the day you kidnapped the president of the UFO Society!"

I pointed to a glass cubicle. "It's coming from in there!"

"That's the office of the Under-Pant in charge of visitors!" Stan exclaimed.

I threw open the door. There stood our teacher, red-faced and yelling at an important-looking Pant behind a tall desk.

"Earth will make you pay for this!" roared Mr. Slomin. "We invented the space shuttle and peel-and-stick postage stamps. We'll figure out a way to get even with you!"

The Under-Pant was laughing so hard that he could barely keep from falling off his chair. "Earth?" he croaked. "Do you spell that with a U?" Finally, he managed to get his trembling finger up to his nasal processor. "Ah, here it is. Earth—an extremely distant and unimportant planet, known for its high-quality traffic jams and allergies, and a race of extremely intelligent dogs who know great knock-knock jokes. Class: Q."

WELCOME tO Urth.

I could almost see smoke shooting out of our teacher's ears. "We're *not* Q-class!!" he roared. "Earth is Class A, all the way!" He bolted out of the office and raced down the hall.

Chapter 10

PANTS·PORTATION

"Mr. Slomin!" I cried. "Come back!"

I grabbed Stan and the two of us shot down the corridor after our teacher. We rounded the corner just in time to see him burst out of the spaceport building and into the street.

"After him!" I cried.

Stan and I galloped through the exit. Instantly, I bounced off some guy and got knocked flying. It's a good thing they carpeted the whole planet or I probably would have brained myself.

I tried to get up. It was impossible. Dozens of people stepped over me, knocking me down again. Pants brushed by to the left and right. This place was *packed*! And everybody was dressed in white shirts and polka-dot ties. Their fingers bobbed in and out of their noses.

JUST LiKE THE MaLL aT ChrisTMas.

I was in Nose Picker Land!

The kids in my class who were so grossed out by Stan—Calista, Tanner, and the others—they'd *croak* if they saw Pan! They wouldn't know who to make fun of first.

A hand reached down and pulled me up. It was Stan.

Desperately, I scanned the sea of Pants around us. "Where's Mr. Slomin? Where did all these aliens come from?"

He looked cross. "Devin, you're on Pan now. *We're* not aliens. *You* are."

I wracked my brain. "Fungus! He can track anything!" I put two fingers in my mouth and whistled. Good old Fungus came running. But when I sent him out into the crowd, he got into a conversation with the first Pant he ran into.

"Not that guy!" I cried. "Find Mr. Slomin! Aww—"

"All those years on Earth he's had nobody to talk to," Stan reminded me. "He's probably saved up a lot to say."

I had one last chance. I took a deep breath and bellowed, "Stop that earthling!!"

Instantly, two sets of arms grabbed me from behind.

"Consider yourself stopped," came the voice of Zgrbnys over my left shoulder. "Thanks to brilliant quick thinking by me."

"Excuse me," countered Gthrmnys over my right, "*I* stopped him first."

"No, *I* stopped him first."

"Not *me*!" I howled. "The *other* earthling! Mr. Slomin!"

Zgrbnys glared at me. "Smarty-Pants execute instructions exactly and perfectly. If you want someone to read your mind, call the Seersuckers."

"They give away free lollipops," added Gthrmnys, as the two walked off in a huff.

"It's too late now," I moaned. "We'll never find Mr. Slomin in this crazy crowd. Oh, man, we broke Rule 4!"

"Rule 4?" questioned Stan.

"**Always stay on your teacher's good side,**" I explained miserably. "You know, joke around with him, volunteer for school plays and stuff. And—oh, yeah—**don't get him lost on a strange planet!**" I looked around frantically. "Aw, man, now Fungus is gone, too! This place is nuts! Why is everybody so frantic?"

Stan shrugged. "Remember, we Pants have only two weeks in the office to store up fifty weeks of vacation time. We have to work incredibly hard. See? There are Suit Pants rushing to meetings; Short Pants on their way to school. Look—" He pointed. "There are the Fire Pants battling a blaze with their Panty-Hose. Everybody is busy on Pan."

REGULAR OR CONTROL-TOP?

"What about those guys?" I asked. Several young Pants sat right in the middle of the carpeted street. "They don't look busy to me. I think half of them are asleep."

"Oh, those are the Slacks," Stan explained. "They're the laziest citizens of Pan. They've turned off their nasal processors and gone back to a simpler way of life. They relax all day, eating the many loitering tickets the Police Pants give them."

My head was spinning. I had to calm down. It's easy to start thinking of Pan as a big joke because of Under-Pants, Panty-Hoses, the Big Zipper, and junk like that. But there was nothing funny about Earth's future being on the line.

I thought back to my Rules of Coolness.

☞ **Rule 15:** When you've got a million things to do, focus on the most important one.

Sure, we had to find Fungus and Mr. Slomin. But a fat lot of good that would do us if we couldn't save Earth. That had to be Job One.

"How do we get in to see the Grand Pant?" I asked Stan.

"We have to go to the Planetary Bureau," Stan

explained. "That's where the government is."

"Okay," I said. "Where's your car?"

"Car?" Stan repeated. "There are no motor vehicles on Pan."

I frowned. "Then how are you supposed to get anywhere?"

"In a Jumper." Stan led me down an alley away from the crowd. My eyes fell on a small, velvet-covered sofa right next to a sign that said PANTS-PORTATION.

I took a seat beside Stan on the couch. "This is pretty cool," I told him. "On Earth you have to stand while waiting for the bus. When does the Jumper come?"

"It's already here," Stan replied.

I looked around. "No, it isn't. There's nothing here but this cou—"

Suddenly, our sofa launched itself straight up. With a soft whistling sound, it soared a thousand feet in the air. The speed was dizzying. I felt like my stomach was down around my socks.

I'm amazed I didn't throw up.

Chapter 11

#1 THE BELTWAY

"*A*aaaaaaaaah!!" I shrieked.

"Sorry," said my exchange buddy. "I, Stan, should have remembered that Earth furniture is the nonflying kind."

"Don't they have seat belts on these things?" I rasped. If I fell off this couch, there wouldn't be enough left of me to send home in a test tube!

"Destination?" came a voice from the armrest.

"Planetary Bureau," said Stan.

And we hurtled forward at ninety miles an hour. My stomach shifted from my socks to the back of my throat.

I had to admit the view was pretty nice—pink sky, orange mountains, yellow lakes, red canyons.

73

I pointed. "Hey, look! You've got the Goodyear Blimp on Pan!"

"Not exactly," replied Stan, tight-lipped.

As we passed by the big balloon, I was able to read the sign on the side: VISIT BEAUTIFUL MERCURY.

"Shakespeare!" I muttered under my breath.

From high up, I could see dozens of that cheater's billboards all over Levi-Strauss. COME TO MERCURY—IT'S LIKE A SAUNA OUT HERE; MERCURY—NUMBER ONE UNDER THE SUN; LET YOUR BLOOD BOIL ON MERCURY. Wherever we went, an annoying jingle played over and over:

A hot rock with a cool view,
Mercury's the place for you.

And then we were dropping out of the pink sky—a thousand feet straight down. I recontacted my stomach on the way.

Just when it seemed like we were about to be smashed into a million pieces, our Jumper slowed down and we got off the couch and stepped into the carpeted street.

I was so dizzy that I fell on my face three times before my head finally cleared.

We were right in front of a huge building: #1 The Beltway. Carved in the stone wall was E PANTIBUS ZIP'EM.

"'Out of many Pants, one Big Zipper,'" Stan translated. "That's the motto of our planet."

I felt a little shiver. If Earth was going to be saved, it would be right here. This was the place, and now was the moment.

It's a big deal to get an appointment with the Grand Pant. You have to fill out a lot of forms. Stan came back from the clerk with a wheelbarrow full of paper.

"You've got to be kidding," I grumbled. "Mr. Slomin doesn't give this much homework in a year."

"Don't be such a sofa turnip," Stan chided. "Okay, here's question one: What is your shoe size?"

I blew my stack. "Shoe size? What do they need to know *that* for? You don't even *wear* shoes on Pan!"

"Devin, this is for the Grand Pant!" Stan exclaimed. "Do you think it would be easy to get in to see a president or a prime minister on Earth?"

"Oh, all right," I groaned. "Size six."

"I, Stan, am a size four. Question two: Why are manhole covers round? That's a trick question. Only the Smarty-Pants, the Under-Pants, and the Grand Pant himself know that."

"What about Zgrbnys and Gthrmnys?" I challenged. "They blanked on it on *Jeopardy!*"

Stan ignored me. "Question three: Do you suffer from bad breath, jock itch, hangnails, or athlete's foot?"

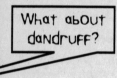

Heart sinking, I dug deep into the wheelbarrow and pulled out the very bottom sheet.

Question 400: In your own words, explain everything that's happened in your entire life. (You may write on the back if you need more space.)

After three very long hours, we pushed our wheelbarrow to the office of the Under-Pant in charge of forms.

This guy was huge. I mean, we've got some

pretty husky people on Earth, but the Under-Pant in charge of forms was like a water bed in a white dress shirt and polka-dot tie.

"Now, that's what I call an Extra-Large Pant," I whispered to Stan.

The Under-Pant stuck his head in our wheelbarrow and took an enormous bite out of the paper stack.

HE NEEDS TO gO ON a diET—aLL tracING PaPEr.

"No-o-o-o-o-o!" I sprang forward to save our work.

But the guy must have been part vacuum cleaner, too. He just kept stuffing his face. By the time I finally managed to pull the wheelbarrow away, it was empty.

I was enraged. "Why did you eat all our forms?"

He rolled his eyes at me. "What did you expect me to do—read them?"

"Yeah!"

He was shocked. "But I'd starve! Besides, if I read the forms, I'd have to let people in to see the Grand Pant."

"But isn't that the whole point of your job?" asked Stan.

"Oh, no," the Under-Pant said seriously. "My job is to keep people away from the Grand Pant. He never sees anybody. He's far too important."

"But this is an emergency!" Stan pleaded. "A whole planet's future is at stake."

"Oh, all right," sighed the Under-Pant. He stuck a pudgy finger up his nose. Come back at four-thirty—"

"Hooray!" I cheered.

"On May sixth," the water bed went on.

"*May sixth?!*"

"In the year 2168," the Under-Pant finished.

There was a polite knock at the door.

"Forsooth," came a voice. "Might I poppeth in to see His Most Tailored Majesty?"

The big Under-Pant leaped to his feet. "Sir! May the Crease be with you! What an honor! Go right in!"

"Wait a minute!" I exploded. "How come *he* doesn't have to wait till 2168?"

Then I got a look at the guy in the doorway. Round face, clipped beard, all that forsooth stuff. The newcomer was none other than *Shakespeare!*

I instantly thought of about ten new Rules of

Coolness just by looking at him. Stuff like: Don't wear leotards, and Pointy slippers are for elves. This guy put the double *E* in "dweeb."

I grabbed that sneak by his white ruffled collar. "You dirty rotten low-down back-stabbing crook—"

He addressed Stan. "Greetings, Agent Mflxnys. And this young knave must be Devin Hunter." Playfully, he reached over and poked at the garage-door opener on my belt. He laughed. "Thy device remindeth me of Earth. It looketh pretty, but it doeth nothing."

Stan spoke up. "Agent Shkprnys, you promised Earth an extension. Yet you traveled to Pan and closed the deal for Mercury. I, Stan, don't understand."

Shakespeare shrugged. "I remembereth not any extension."

"Liar, liar, pants on fire!" I shouted. "You double-crosser! What about 'To thine own self be true'?"

That rotten Shakespeare laughed right in my face. "To mine own self I was true, earthling. Thine own self is thy problem." And he waltzed straight through the door and in to see the Grand Pant.

I grabbed Stan and tried to follow, but the Under Pant in charge of forms blocked our way. We bounced off that water bed stomach like a couple of Ping-Pong balls.

"Aw, come on!" I wailed. "You let Shakespeare through!"

"Shkprnys is a legend," the Under-Pant explained.

"Devin is considered a legend on Earth," Stan wheedled.

"Yeah . . . I . . . won a lot of merit badges in Cub Scouts!" I blustered.

"How can you two compare yourselves to Shkprnys the One and Only?" the Under-Pant said scornfully. "You're barely out of kindergarten."

"Kindergarten?" I cried. "Stan is 147 years old!"

"Exactly," the Under-Pant said smugly. "On Pan, kindergarten lasts until you turn ninety. You don't get out of diapers before your twenty-first birthday."

Boy, was I mad. I'm not usually a mean person. But if I didn't blow off steam, my head was going to explode. I narrowed my eyes and said the cruelest thing I could think of to a big-shot Pant. **"You're so dumb that I'll bet you don't even know why manhole covers are round!"**

Stan shot me a horrified look, but I didn't care. If my planet was going out past Pluto, I had more important problems than insulting a water bed.

All at once, the Under-Pant threw his huge head into his chubby arms and started *sobbing*!

"I'm ruined!" he howled. "It was only a matter of time before people found out!"

I guess Pants take their manhole covers pretty seriously.

Chapter 12
FILET OF PHONE BOOK

Stan was shocked. "You don't know, *either*?"

"You can't threaten me!" the big Under-Pant blubbered. "Go ahead! Tell the whole planet! I still won't let you in to see the Grand Pant!"

He outweighed us by a couple of tons. What could we do? We got out of there.

When we were back on the crowded Beltway, I turned to Stan. "Now what?"

His fried-egg eyes looked tragic. "Only the Grand Pant has the power to change the decision to pick Mercury. I, Stan, am sorry, Devin."

I was horrified. "You mean there's no chance for Earth?"

At that moment, a small wooden stick came sailing through the air and hit me right in the chest.

"Woof!" came a gruff voice.

Through the crowd barreled a burly figure in a St. Louis Cardinals baseball uniform. He ran right up to us and snatched the stick off the carpet. It was Mark McGwire.

"Mgwrnys!" exclaimed Stan. "What are you doing?"

"Staying in shape in the off-season," replied the home run king. "My new trainer suggested fetching sticks."

"What new trainer?" I asked suspiciously.

"Your dog, Fungus," he explained. "He had a lot of great exercises for me. Too bad there aren't any fire hydrants here on Pan. Hey, how come you guys look so upset?"

BasebaLL is goiNg to the dogs.

Sadly, Stan told him about Shakespeare's double-crossing. "And now we can't get an appointment to see the Grand Pant. We can't even get a message to him."

The great slugger shrugged. "*I* can."

"How?" I asked.

McGwire reached into his duffel bag and took out his bat and a baseball. He handed the ball to Stan. "Got a pen?"

Stan wrote:

> **Your Most Tailored Majesty,**
>
> **Agent Shkprnys cheated! Earth is still in the running for resort planet. I promise to explain everything tomorrow.**
>
> **Your faithful travel agent on Earth,**
>
> **Agent Mflxnys**
>
> **P.S. Urgent!**

I still didn't get it. "But how are you going to send this ball to the Grand Pant?"

"His Most Tailored Majesty lives in the penthouse of the Planetary Bureau," McGwire explained. He drew back his bat and tossed the ball up in front of him.

POW!

On Earth it would have been a seven-thousand-foot home run. The ball took off like a rocket. It soared high up the side of the building until I lost it in the pink sky. And then—

CRASH!!!

Stan went white to the ears. "You broke the Grand Pant's window!"

Quickly, the home run king packed his bat away. "If anybody asks," he mumbled, "I never left Earth." And he shouldered his duffel and disappeared into the crowd.

"Don't worry," I told Stan. "I broke Roscoe's window once. It wasn't too expensive."

He looked nervous. "But the Grand Pant's window was a gift from the legendary frosted glassmakers of the Milky Way."

PEOPLE WhO LiVE iN glass hOUSES ShOULdN'T gET ELECTEd Grand PANT.

"Oh—well, baseball players make a lot of money." I changed the subject. "Come on, let's look for Fungus and Mr. Slomin, okay?"

"Soon," promised my exchange buddy. "Right now, I, Stan, require food."

All at once, I realized I was starving, too. We hadn't eaten anything since dinner before the Smarty-Pants went on *Jeopardy!* It seemed like a year ago.

"Okay, let's eat." I frowned. "Do they have Burger King on Pan?"

Stan put his finger up his nose. "We're in luck, Devin! Can you believe that we're here during the two weeks my mother isn't on vacation? She's a fantastic cook."

So we grabbed another Jumper—a love seat with flowery throw cushions. We flew to Stan's house in the Capri District. This time I only fell down once after we landed. I was kind of proud of myself for that.

Stan stuck his nose in the lock at 28 Inseam Avenue. There was a click, and the door swung wide.

"Mom?"

Their reunion was pretty emotional. On Earth it would have broken a few of my Rules of Coolness. But when you get to be 147, I guess you've earned the right to dweeb it up a little when you see your mom after a long trip.

Finally, the mushy stuff was over, and I got my first good look at Mrs. Mflxnys. I did a double take.

"Stan!" I blurted. **"Your mother looks exactly like the Mona Lisa!"**

"She *is* the Mona Lisa," Stan said seriously.

"What?!"

"I mean she was the model for the 'Mona Lisa,'" Stan amended. "She was on Earth as a Training Pant even before Shakespeare."

"But how did you get to be the Mona Lisa?" I asked Stan's mom. "Did you win a contest?"

Mrs. Mflxnys laughed. "I was stationed in a country called Italy. One day, a very nice man named Leonardo da Vinci asked if he could paint my portrait, and—" She gave me a half smile. "And it came out quite well."

"Quite well?" I cried. "Every kid on Earth has to learn about that picture for art class! It's the most famous painting of all time!"

"Devin," Stan chuckled. "the 'Mona Lisa' is a very nice try for an earthling artist. But naturally, one of the Painter Pants could do a much better job with his nasal processor."

I had to agree that nasal processors were pretty handy gadgets. That gave me an idea. "Hey, Stan, while we're on Pan, do you think *I* could get a nose computer? I mean, eighty-five thousand light-years is a long way. I wouldn't want to leave without a souvenir."

Stan looked bewildered. "Where would you put a nasal processor?"

I shrugged. "Up my schnoz, same as you."

"That's impossible," Stan told me. "An earthling's head is filled with brains, so there's no room for anything else."

"Don't Pants have brains?" I asked.

"Of course. Two of them," said Stan. "They're behind our knees."

> Call the orthopedist.
> I need brain surgery.

"Let's have dinner," suggested Mrs. Mflxnys.

Hooray! Boy, was I famished. "I could eat a horse!" I promised Stan.

He didn't get the joke. "Why would you ingest a large equestrian mammal?"

But when we got to the kitchen, I realized the joke was on me. Heaping plates of food covered the table. It was all paper.

"What *is* this?" I heaved.

"A meal fit for a king-sized Pant!" crowed Stan. "Filet of phone book with fountain-pen ink gravy. Stir-fried newsprint with cardboard florets. And for dessert, Dictionary Delight with confetti sprinkles and white-out sauce on the side."

I gagged.

Chapter 13

TWELVE THOUSAND
NEW E·MAILS

Let's just say that I didn't eat a really big dinner. Paper isn't my idea of a tasty treat. Mostly, I just pushed the stuff around my plate to make it look smaller. I'm kind of an expert at that from liver night at my own house.

But for Stan, it was his first home cooking since he'd left for Earth. He was like a starving shark. Even after Mrs. Mflxnys had gone to bed, he sat at the table, attacking his fourth helping of Dictionary Delight.

> What a SWEET tooth.

I was worried. "You know, Stan, even if we do get in to see the Grand Pant tomorrow, why should he believe us? We can't prove Shakespeare cheated."

"We'll just have to show him that Earth is the superior planet," Stan mumbled, his mouth full of paper shreds. "If only we had done our social studies project! Then we'd have lots of terrific things to say about Earth and the human race."

"We need Mr. Slomin," I said earnestly. "He's a social studies expert. Maybe we should check the newspapers to see if there's a story about a nut-job earthling running around town."

"Devin," Stan chided me, "we could never have newspapers on Pan. They'd be eaten before anyone could even read the headlines. We get our

news from a vast computer web of information."

"You mean the Internet?" I asked.

He chuckled. "On Pan, we use the Internet to pass notes in preschool. I, Stan, am talking about the Overall. It's the network of every single nasal processor on Pan."

He stuck his finger up his nose. "Access the Overall." He frowned. "Uh-oh. I, Stan, have twelve thousand new E-mails to read. That's what I get for traveling to the other side of the galaxy."

"Never mind that," I said sternly. "Is there anything about an earthling on the loose? And maybe an Earth dog? If I go home without Fungus, I may as well not go home."

"Hmmm." Stan frowned. "All the chat rooms are clogged up with stories about a hilarious new street comedian. They've nicknamed him the Clown Pant."

"Have you ever heard of this guy?" I asked.

"He just started appearing today," Stan replied, twisting his finger as he worked his nose computer. "He shows up somewhere and does a routine that has everyone rolling on the carpet. Then he disappears just as suddenly. No one even knows his real name. Wait a minute—I'm getting a message."

He ran over and plugged his nose into a socket. There was a flicker, and then the entire wall turned into a giant TV screen.

The picture was fuzzy at first, but the figure of a man slowly started to come into focus.

"Mr. Slomin?" I asked the giant-sized image that was blurring all around us.

The picture became clearer. My heart sank. It wasn't our teacher. In fact, it was the last guy in the universe I wanted to see just then.

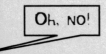

Oh, NO!

Chapter 14
DOUBLE-CROSSETHED!

My most *un*favorite Pant—Shakespeare.

"O Agent Mflxnys, Agent Mflxnys, wherefore art thou, Agent Mflxnys?"

Stan stepped out into the middle of the room. "Here I am, Agent Shkprnys."

"Forsooth! May the Crease be with thee!"

"May a runaway asteroid make a crease in your ugly face," I muttered under my breath. I'm not the forgiving type.

Even Stan was pretty fed up with Shakespeare by this time. "I, Stan, realize that you are a Pant whose belt loops would be hard to fill. But we're very upset at how you tricked us."

"I knoweth this," said Shakespeare sadly from the wall. "Methinks I feel like a cad. I shall maketh this contest fair again."

"How?" asked Stan.

"Forsooth," he replied, "the Grand Pant is a personal friend. On the morrow, when the clock striketh noon, come to the Planetary Bureau, and I shall gettest thee a meeting with His Most Tailored Majesty."

Stan glowed with happiness. "Oh, Agent Shkprnys, I, Stan, am sorry I ever doubted you. You truly are the One and Only! Thank you so much!"

"Mentioneth it not," said Shakespeare. "Until the morrow then. Forsooth!"

He faded out, and THE ENDE appeared on the wall.

"I don't trust him," I declared. "Not after he bamboozled us like that."

"Relax," Stan insisted. "He said he was sorry."

I was still nervous. Rule 32 says: **If a guy burns you once, don't give him a chance to do it again.**

But we had to go along with Shakespeare's plan. After all, what choice did we have?

We stayed up half the night searching the Overall for Fungus and Mr. Slomin. We found nothing. What lousy luck that this Clown Pant guy showed up at exactly the same time we did! Nobody wanted to talk about anything else.

In the morning, we said good-bye to Mrs. Mflxnys.

"I'm so glad you boys found me at home," she told us. "I leave for another vacation today. I've got the most exciting trip planned. I'm going to Mercury."

Farewell, Mona!

"*Mercury?*" we chorused.

"It was discovered by Shkprnys himself," she gushed. "I can't wait to see the rings of Saturn!"

"Aw, Mom," Stan whined. "Why did you have to pick *there*? Can't you go back to the Horsehead Nebula for the annual Naysayers Convention? Or what about the Ring Nebula? It's very shiny this time of year."

She gave him that famous Mona Lisa half smile. "It's too late. I've already snorted my ticket."

"Well, all right," Stan told her. "But I, Stan, wouldn't count on that view of Saturn. **There just might be a big blue planet in the way!**"

On the jump back to town on a leather sofa bed, I was really nervous. I didn't trust

97

Shakespeare as far as I could throw him. I was pretty sure he wasn't going to show up.

But as our Jumper set us down in front of the Planetary Bureau, there he was, ruffled collar, leotard and all. He was waving at us and calling something. What was he saying?

"Forsooth! There they are! The vile knaves who broketh the Grand Pant's window! **Arresteth them!**"

Police Pants were running at us from all directions. Before I knew it, we were both in handcuffs.

"I'm a cuffed Pant," Stan said in disbelief.

I was so mad I could hardly see straight. "I'll get you for this," I seethed at Shakespeare.

He laughed in my face. "I quaketh with fear, earthling. Forsooth, a planetary tug-ship is already in the Pan-Ama Canal on its way to taketh Earth out past Pluto. When the clock striketh three, thy planet shall be a large blue Popsicle."

I stuck out my jaw. "I read *Romeo and Juliet*," I growled. "It really, really stank."

Chapter 15

TWO HUNDRED YEARS IN PRISON

"Well, I can't believe it's come to this," I said miserably. "We're in jail."

"We Pants call it the Planetary Holster," Stan informed me.

"Holster, hoosegow, slammer." I moaned. "It's still jail."

I turned blazing eyes on Stan. "Why can't Police Pants take fingerprints like everybody else?"

"Nose-printing is a far more efficient way to keep track of criminals on Pan," Stan explained.

What happens if you get a NOSE job?

I scrubbed at the black ink on my nose. "It's pretty embarrassing, you know!" Until you have to bend over and press your schnoz on an ink pad, you don't know what it is to feel like an idiot.

A Pan jail isn't very much like an Earth prison. There are no bars and no cells. It seems like you could just make a break for it. But the prison uniform is a wide metal belt. If you try to escape, you get sucked back by a giant magnet in the rear of the holding cell.

"We'll get out of here," Stan promised. "We have to if we're going to save Earth."

"What's the point of saving Earth?" I grumbled. **"When my parents find out I was in jail, it'll be the end of the world anyway."**

"All right, you menaces to society!" called the sergeant. "Lunch!"

A metal tray came clattering across the cement floor.

Our only fellow prisoner, an old Pant named Quxfthnys, took a bite and gagged. "Blecch! This is cruel and unusual punishment! How do they expect us to eat this garbage?"

He slid the tray over to Stan, who made a face. "It's inhuman. It's un-Pant, even."

I peered over Stan's shoulder. My eyes nearly

popped out of my head. A mountain of chili nachos towered over a piping hot pepperoni and double-cheese pizza. French fries and onion rings surrounded three hamburgers with the works. For dessert there was a giant gooey chocolate cake. And best of all, not a piece of paper in sight.

I'm not embarrassed to say I ate like a pig.

Stan was horrified. "Devin, how can you think about food at a time like this?"

I'M gETtINg huNgry jUST reADiNg it!

"I'm starving," I defended myself between mouthfuls. "Remember, I can't just dump out a filing cabinet and chow down like you."

"It's almost two o'clock! The tug-ship is barely an hour away from Earth!" He snatched up the metal tray, sending onion rings flying.

"Hey!" I snapped. "I wasn't finished yet!"

My exchange buddy dumped out the rest of lunch and banged the tray on the floor. "Sergeant!" he yelled. "When do we get our bail hearing?"

"Pipe down in there!" the sergeant ordered. "We have to wait for the Under-Pant in charge of forms to come over and eat your paperwork."

"But we've got to get to the Planetary Bureau!" Stan protested. "It's urgent!"

"You should have thought of that before breaking the Grand Pant's window!" the sergeant shot right back.

"You broke the Grand Pant's window?" asked Quxfthnys. "Wow! I'm a small-time crook compared with you. I'm only here for wearing shoes on a public carpet."

Miserably, we sat there in the slammer, watching Earth's final hour tick away. Two-

fifteen. Two-thirty. I wondered if I'd ever see my house again. And if I did, would it be frozen into a block of ice on a dark, frostbitten planet?

"All right!" barked the sergeant. "Mflxnys and Hunter. You're charged with destroying the personal property of the Grand Pant. This crime carries a penalty of two hundred years in prison."

My giant lunch lurched in my stomach. *"Two hundred years?!"*

Stan raised his hand. "Uh, sir? Could my friend possibly get an earthling discount? Humans don't live two hundred years."

> IF YOU CAN'T DO THE TIME, DON'T DO THE CRIME.

"That's no excuse!" snapped the sergeant. "Fruit flies only live two weeks, but we just sentenced one to ten years for buzzing around the Grand Pant's watermelon. Now—how do you plead?"

"Not guilty!" I squeaked. "It was Mark McGwire!"

That broke Rule 9: **Never rat out your friends.** I'll make it up to you, Mr. McGwire. I'll let my dog turn you into a *star*.

"Let's see what you say after a few hours of interrogation," he snarled.

Interrogation! I didn't like the sound of that. Were we going to be tortured? Beside me, Stan was starting to sweat.

The sergeant reached for me, and I almost jumped out of my skin. But he was only unlocking my metal belt. "All right, Earthling," he growled, "*promise* you won't try to escape."

I frowned. Promise? "Oh, sure," I said. "I promise."

"I promise, too," added Stan readily.

And he freed us. I was amazed. If Earth ran its jails this way, they'd be empty.

As the sergeant marched us through the halls of the Holster, I whispered to Stan. "Get ready to make a run for it!"

Stan was appalled. "But, Devin! We *promised*!"

"And he believed us," I chortled. "What a chump!"

"But a Pant's word of honor is even more important than his nose!" Stan protested.

"Earth is more important than anything!" I hissed. I looked around. "This place is crawling

with Police Pants. How can we create a diver-
sion?"

At that very moment, one of the younger
cops pointed out the window. "Hey, look, everybody! It's the Clown Pant!"

Pandemonium broke loose. People were cheering and patting each other on the back. Then
every single Police Pant in the building stampeded
straight out the front door.

Quxfthnys was hot on their heels. "Come on,

guys!" he called to us. "It's the Clown Pant! He's the funniest Pant in the universe!" He joined the rush, but two feet from the exit, his metal prison belt got too far from the giant magnet. With a *zap*, he was yanked back to the cell like a dog who has run out of leash. "Twill!" he exclaimed dejectedly.

Stan started to follow the Police Pants into the crowd of onlookers that had formed around the famous comedian.

I grabbed his arm. "What are you, nuts? Let's get out of here!"

"But it's the Clown Pant!" he cried.

I was furious. "I don't care if it's the whole circus! *Run!*"

"Devin, *look!*"

He got an arm around my shoulders and wheeled me about. I gawked. I goggled. I almost died.

It was the Clown Pant, all right. He stood at the center of a huge cheering crowd of adoring fans. Was he a jovial entertainer with a million-dollar smile? No way! He wasn't even a Pant!

He was Mr. Slomin!

REALLY?

Chapter 16

A WEREWOLVES CONVENTION

I couldn't believe my eyes. *Mr. Slomin?!*

"How could Mr. Slomin be a comedian?" I asked in amazement. "He isn't funny! He never even smiles—not unless he's giving somebody six months of detentions."

Then the famous and celebrated Clown Pant began his comedy routine.

"A terrible revenge is coming!" declared Mr. Slomin, his face bright red. "It's coming from the planet Earth!"

The crowd roared with laughter.

"What's so hilarious about that?" I asked Stan.

Stan looked apologetic. "Well, I, Stan, love Earth, but it *is* Q-class, and—no offense—couldn't fight its way out of its own atmosphere."

I was still too shocked to be insulted.

Mr. Slomin was just getting warmed up. "Right now the armies of all the great nations are combining into an invasion force!"

The laughter swelled like someone had bumped up the volume. A loud guffaw escaped Stan. He tried to cover it up as a cough.

"I'm sorry." He chuckled. "But no planet has *armies* anymore. **That's so second millennium.**"

"One of these days," promised Mr. Slomin, waving his arms like a wild man, "your skies will darken with our stealth bombers, AWACs, smart bombs, and cruise missiles!"

Well, that must have been the most hilarious joke of all. Those Pants hurled themselves down on the rug and howled. It sounded like a werewolves convention during a full moon. Even Stan couldn't hold back a pretty big laugh.

"Let me guess," I said sarcastically. "Cruise missiles are out of style, too?"

Duh.

"No, we still use them," he gasped, wiping the tears from his eyes. "To deliver Chinese menus! Oh, this is so funny!"

"Well, the show's over," I said firmly. "We've got to get Mr. Slomin to the Planetary Bureau. He's the only guy who can tell the Grand Pant all the great things about Earth."

As Mr. Slomin's hysterical audience rolled around on the carpet, we tiptoed through the crowd. I accidentally kicked one guy in the head, but he was laughing so hard, I don't think he even noticed.

ALL the world LOVES a CLOWN.

"Cruise missiles!" he wheezed. "What are they going to attack us with? Chop suey?"

"Hold the noodles on mine!" wailed a lady next to him.

Mr. Slomin was still raving. "We'll show you who's a Q-class planet! We're class A, all the way! We're gonna—"

"Mr. Slomin!" I called. "Over here!"

"Devin!" Our teacher pulled me aside. "It's going to be easy for Earth to fight these aliens. They're morons. All they do is laugh. What a bunch of saps."

Poor Mr. Slomin. He honestly thought that Earth was going to war because Pan had kidnapped the president of the Clearview UFO Society.

"There's a better way!" I pleaded. "We're going to take you to a man called the Grand Pant. Can you tell him everything that's great about Earth and the human race?"

"Of course. I'm a social studies teacher." He dropped his voice to a whisper. "But is it wise to give them too much information about Earth? They could use it against us in the war."

"What war?" Stan asked in confusion. "How could Earth ever attack Pan? Earth doesn't even know that Pan exists; it has no way to reach Pan; and the odds of Earth defeating Pan are six trillion trillion to one. That would be harder than winning all fifty of your state lotteries and being stung to death by bees on the same day."

"You're just trying to scare Earth out of kicking your butts!" Mr. Slomin told Stan.

"If you can convince the Grand Pant how great Earth is," I insisted, "Earth will be in no danger from anything." I turned to the crowd. "Okay, folks, the show's over!" I announced.

"Go home and eat some Kleenex or something."

We got a standing ovation as we made our escape down the carpeted street, dragging Mr. Slomin along with us. I looked at my watch. Two-forty-five! **The tug-ship would be at Earth in only *fifteen minutes!***

"But, Devin," Stan protested as we ran, "how are we going to get in to see the Grand Pant? We don't have an appointment, remember?"

"We'll get in," I promised through clenched teeth. "Trust me."

At the Planetary Bureau, we strode right past the suckers filling out tons of paperwork. We stormed straight into the office of the Under-Pant in charge of forms.

The extra-large Pant leaped up and blocked the door when he saw us. "You again?" he sneered.

I had never felt so determined. I was an irresistible force of nature, like a tornado. "Out of my way, Jumbo!" I roared. "We're going in there, and nothing's going to stop us!"

"Hah!" The big Pant's many chins vibrated with the booming of his voice. "What makes you think you're important enough to get a meeting with the Grand Pant?"

"Not *me*!" I exclaimed, putting an arm around Mr. Slomin's shoulders. "Don't you know who this is? Stand aside, Water Bed, and make way for the one and only Clown Pant!"

Chapter 17

THE GREAT
MILLENNIAL VAULT

"The Clown Pant?" The Under-Pant in charge of forms straightened his back and snapped a military salute which ended with his middle finger up his nose. A fifteen-foot-high door opened and he bellowed. "Sire, the fabulous and incomparable Clown Pant has come to perform for you!"

Stan was blown away. "This is it, Devin!" he hissed, pointing inside. "The Hanger!"

I frowned. "Why do they call it the Hanger?"

"It's where all the most important Pants hang out," Stan explained with awe and respect.

If you took a giant movie theater and covered every seat and every wall with gleaming gold leaf, then you'd have something that looked like the Hanger. The place was packed with Pants—

an ocean of white dress shirts and polka-dot ties. We were fixed in the stare of a thousand fried-egg eyes.

"Look," Stan whispered. "It's the Cabinet of Under-Pants, next to the Smarty-Pants Council of Wisdom. On the left, those are the Pedal Pushers and the Sweat Pants. Together, they're in charge of physical fitness for the whole planet. Now look to your right. Those are the Bell Bottoms, who sound the alarm in times of crisis. The Baggy Pants handle garbage disposal and carpet cleaning. The Parachute Pants forecast the weather for the Cargo Pants, who make sure all shipments and packages get where they're going. The Ski Pants control the polar regions. Beside the Press Gallery, where the Pressed Pants do their reporting, you'll see the Designer Jeans. They all have the same name, Devin. If you go to their office and call out, 'Hey, Jean,' every single one of them will come running. And there at the front"—his voice quivered with emotion—"is His Most Tailored Majesty, the Grand Pant."

That's ENOUgh PONtS tO OPEN a taiLor shOp!

I gawked in amazement. Not at the

Grand Pant. I mean, if you've seen one dweeb in a polka-dot tie, you've seen them all. But there, right at the great man's side, sat Fungus!

"Fungus!" I snapped. "Bad dog! I've been worried sick about you!"

The Grand Pant leaned over and barked something at Fungus.

"He's asking if Fungus is your owner," translated Stan.

"I'm *his* owner!" I snapped. "Dogs don't own people; people own dogs."

The Grand Pant frowned. "Hmmm. I thought dogs were in charge on Earth, followed by parakeets, mongooses, caterpillars, moss, and *then* humans."

"It's definitely humans, sire," Stan supplied. "But dogs come in second as man's best friend."

"As well they should," agreed the Grand Pant. "Why, Fungus knows knock-knock jokes that haven't even made it to this part of the galaxy yet." He turned to Mr. Slomin. "But I understand *you* are the master when it comes to jokes, Clown Pant. They say you can make a Pant laugh himself out of his pleats. Entertain us with your vast humor."

"This is it, Mr. Slomin," I urged. "Do it. Tell him how awesome Earth is."

It was just like social studies class. Mr. Slomin talked about the Pyramids, the Great Wall of China, the cathedrals of Europe, and the towering skyscrapers of today. He told the Grand Pant about the "can do" human spirit, from the invention of the wheel to Marco Polo and Columbus and the great voyages of discovery.

Did hE MENTiON thE iNVENTiON OF chEAp jOKES?

He was fantastic! He may have been a UFO freak and the weirdest teacher in school, but today he was my hero. I looked at the Grand Pant. *Nobody* could send us out past Pluto after a speech like this!

The leader of Pan gave a huge yawn. "This guy isn't funny. I haven't laughed once." He stood up. "Guards, remove these earthlings from the Hanger."

Oh, *no*! I checked my watch and freaked out. It was 2:55! The planetary tug would be at Earth in *five minutes*! All was lost! And my family, my town—everything I knew—was headed for the deep freeze!

A Police Pant grabbed me from behind. I shook myself free. I had never been so mad in my entire life. The future of a whole planet was at stake, but did the Grand Pant care? No! He sealed our fate with no more concern than he would give to clipping his toenails!

Well, I just started screaming insults at the guy. "You're a bum! Your mother wears army boots! I hate your guts! You stink! You're so stupid that—that—"

And suddenly, I remembered. Here on Pan, what was the worst thing you could say to somebody? If you really want to hurt a guy, you say, *"You don't even know why manhole covers are round!"*

I have never heard so many gasps of horror all at the same time. The floor shook as the entire government of Pan leaped to its feet in outrage. I thought Stan was going to disintegrate.

The Police Pant grabbed me again. **"How dare you disrespect His Most Tailored Majesty?"**

The outrage on the face of the Grand Pant melted away to reveal a look of deep sadness. "The earthling is right," he admitted after a moment. "I *don't* know why manhole covers are round."

Shock greeted this announcement. Half the government fainted into the arms of the other half. Fingers shot up noses as the Pressed Pants transmitted this breaking news to their bosses.

"What's more," the Grand Pant went on, "*nobody* knows. The secret has been locked away for centuries in the Great Millennial Vault."

All eyes turned to the corner of the Hanger. There stood a faintly glowing safe the size of a washing machine. It was surrounded by a short wooden fence marked PANTS AT WORK.

Stan found his voice at last. "Forgive me, sire, but I, Stan, have been off the planet. Wasn't the Great Millennial Vault supposed to be opened at the coming of the year 2000?"

The Grand Pant nodded. "Yes, but it's stuck,"

he replied. "And the Smarty-Pants aren't clever enough to get it open. Inside lies the answer to the question that has baffled our people for two thousand years."

I went ballistic. "Are you crazy?! **Are you double-crazy?!** Five billion earthlings are going to freeze in two minutes and you people are worried about stupid manhole covers?!"

I admit it. I went nuts. I pulled the garage-door opener off my belt and flung it with all my might at the Grand Pant.

It bounced off his royal nose and landed on the floor. He staggered slightly, and his Most Tailored Toe stepped right on the button.

There was a *bloop!* like a car alarm and—I stared—

With a loud creaking sound, the door of the Great Millennial Vault swung open!

Chapter 18

WHY MANHOLE COVERS ARE ROUND

I couldn't believe it. Pants were thousands of years ahead of us, and yet none of them could crack that vault. But my plain old earthling garage-door remote control just so happened to work on exactly the right frequency! There stood the Great Millennial Vault, door wide open.

Jaws dropped in amazement. Fingers fell out of noses. Man, you could have heard a pin drop in the Hanger at that moment!

The Grand Pant reached into the vault and pulled out a small scroll. He unrolled it and read it. When he looked at me, there were tears in his eyes.

"The smartest of the Smarty-Pants were unable to open that vault," he said emotionally. "What is this miraculous device that has accomplished it so easily?"

"It was invented by an earthling!" I cried. **"Who's about to be frozen in"**—I looked at my watch and almost swallowed my tongue—**"five seconds!!"**

The Grand Pant put his finger up to his nasal processor. "This is a direct order from the First Nose. I am calling the tug-ship back from Earth."

I felt the greatest relief I've ever known. Now I understood what "in the nick of time" meant.

The Grand Pant smiled at me. "Any society that can create such a marvel must never be tampered with. Who knows what they might invent next? Maybe even bread that's already sliced when you buy it at the store."

Or, in the pick of time.

A delighted *Ooooh!* rippled through the crowd.

"Sire!" Stan breathed. "Are you saying that—"

The Grand Pant nodded. "Earth will be Pan's newest vacation resort!"

"Na-a-a-a-ay!!" came an anguished cry.

Down the aisle of the Hanger sprinted Shakespeare. He ran in short, awkward steps, probably because his leotard was too tight.

I couldn't resist gloating a little. "What's the matter, Shakey? Having a rough day? Maybe you rented a blimp and a few thousand billboards all for nothing?"

That big cheater's face was bright red under his pointed beard. "Thy Most Tailored Majesty," he pleaded with his leader. "Forsooth, how canst thou rippeth me off this way?"

The Grand Pant shrugged. "Sorry, Shkprnys. I never did like Mercury. That place has no atmosphere."

And then William Shakespeare had a good old-fashioned temper tantrum, just like any two-year-old on Earth.

"Forsooth!" he wailed, throwing himself to the floor and pounding it with balled-up fists. "No fair! Thou art all a bunch of twill-heads! **This stinketh big-time!** *Now is the winter of our discontent!*"

The Grand Pant looked displeased. "This is

> I want my vacation planet!

124

not the behavior I expect from the greatest travel agent in history."

But Shakespeare was out of control. "Thou art foul knaves who are not worthy of my talents! May thy next vacation be on a runaway asteroid bound for a dark nebula with cheesy hotels and recycled paper!"

"Take him away," the Grand Pant ordered the guards. "It's time for me to speak to all Pant-kind."

While Shakespeare was dragged out kicking

and screaming, the Pants in the Hanger put their fingers up their noses.

"It's the Emergency Coverall Broadcast System," Stan explained around his hand. "Throughout the galaxy, every single Pant has turned on his nasal processor to hear this."

In other words, it was the largest mass nose-pick of all time. **The Galactic Gross-out.**

"Citizens of Pan," the Grand Pant announced, "two thousand years ago, an important secret was lost to us. Today that secret was regained, thanks to a young earthling. Let me share this great truth with all of you. From now on, everyone from the wisest Smarty-Pants to the tiniest Diaper Pants will know the reason manhole covers are round. It's because a round manhole cover can never fall into the hole. No matter which way you turn it, it always fits perfectly."

What?!! Hundreds of Pants and at least one human (me) looked blank. No matter which way you turn it . . . ?

And then the teacher in Mr. Slomin finally came out.

"It's simple geometry," he explained, like he

126

was standing in front of class 4C, and not on the other side of the galaxy. "A square one could be tilted straight up, turned on a slant, and dropped inside. And it's true of every other shape—except a perfect circle. That's why manhole covers are always made round."

I got all excited for that?

A "Big deal!" died on my lips. All those Pants were clapping. And cheering. Some of them were standing on their chairs, screaming with excitement.

"Brilliant! Simply brilliant!" remarked the Grand Pant. "I declare a planetwide holiday. Let's all go on vacation!"

"The Pan-Pan Travel Bureau can start work on some long-weekend getaway specials," Stan added breathlessly.

That's when I must have overloaded. Chalk it up to being a gazillion miles from home. Or maybe it was Earth's close brush with the deep freeze. Whatever the reason, these aliens were driving me crazy. Weren't there any *important* things to think about?

"What's the matter with you people?" I

howled. "You've got spaceships, and nose computers, and the power of the Crease! But what do you waste your lives on? *Manhole covers*, for crying out loud! I mean, who cares? That would be like the president of the United States spending all his time worrying about why the handrail of an escalator always moves just a little bit faster than the part you stand on!"

Dead silence fell in the Hanger. The Grand Pant looked at me with keen interest. "That's true, young earthling," he said with a frown. "The handrail always *does* seem to go faster."

"That's not what I meant—" I began.

But the leader of Pan was lost in thought. "It's a mystery. An enigma. A conundrum. There must be an explanation. But what?"

"This is even more fascinating than manhole covers," said Stan in wonder.

"Smarty-Pants, put your best thinkers on the job," commanded the Grand Pant. "Top-drawer priority. I need the answer as fast as possible, maybe sooner."

"You'll have it within one hundred seventy-five years," guaranteed the head Smarty-Pant.

"And don't lock it in a vault this time!" the Grand Pant said peevishly.

Yeah, I know. They were totally missing the point. But when you're dealing with aliens, you can't always expect them to think the way you do.

That led me to a new rule of coolness, maybe the most important one of all:

☞ **<u>Rule 99:</u>** It takes all kinds to make a galaxy.

Chapter 19
CLASS A, ALL THE WAY

Hyperspace wasn't nearly as scary on the trip back to Earth. In fact, it was kind of fun—like a roller coaster that could go five hundred million miles per second. I'd like to see Space Mountain do that!

Of course, the main reason I enjoyed the trip home was because I was in a good mood. Everybody was. Stan and I were thrilled by the billboard we saw at the entrance to the Pan-Ama Canal:

VISIT EARTH
CLASS A, ALL THE WAY
WEEKEND PACKAGES AVAILABLE
3 DAYS/2 NITES—ONLY 350 PANTALOONS
(Gravity Not Included)
SNORT 1-800-BIG-BLUE

Mark McGwire was happy because Fungus had given him a brand-new off-season workout. Fungus was wagging his tail from two days of nonstop conversation. And Zgrbnys and Gthrmnys were content because they now understood why manhole covers are round.

"I knew it all along," Zgrbnys assured his partner. "I just wanted to see if *you* knew."

"I knew it, too," Gthrmnys defended himself. "I didn't say anything because I didn't want to make *you* feel bad."

"Then why didn't you answer the question on *Jeopardy!*?" I taunted. "Instead, you busted up the show and punched Alex Trebek in the mouth."

Both Smarty-Pants buried their faces in their ties.

"Quiet, earthling," mumbled Zgrbnys. "We are pondering the most difficult problem of the new millennium, the escalator handrail paradox. It is far too complex for your primitive, Q-class mind."

"We're not Q-class," Mr. Slomin insisted, but this time he was smiling. His "Class A, All the

Way" was the new tourist slogan for Earth, and he was pretty proud of that.

And he was extra happy because this trip proved he'd been right all along.

"I *knew* there were UFOs landing on Earth!" he said with deep satisfaction. "I *knew* there were alien races visiting us! Everybody called me crazy, but I knew it was true! When I tell the rest of the UFO Society—"

"Whoa!" I said quickly. "Mr. Slomin, I'm thrilled that you turned out to be right and all that. But this whole thing has to be kept secret."

"Absolutely not!" declared our teacher. "This is the breakthrough the UFO Society has been waiting for! We're going to put this story on the front page of every newspaper in the world!"

"But then Stan would get arrested!" I protested. **"The Air Force would do all kinds of—like—experiments on him!"**

Mr. Slomin folded his arms. "I can't let that stand in the way of the UFO Society," he said stubbornly.

Oh, *no*! Just when it seemed like we were out of the woods, here was a terrible dilemma.

"What are we going to do?" I whispered to Stan.

"Devin," he chided me, "don't panic. We have two Smarty-Pants with us. And they're even smarter than before because now they know why manhole covers are round." He turned to Zgrbnys and Gthrmnys in the pilots' chairs. "Can you use your mega-intelligence to think of a way to stop Mr. Slomin?"

"Naturally," said Zgrbnys. "We will focus a beam of pure energy to scatter the molecules of his brain over a million light-years of deep space."

"And," continued Gthrmnys, "we will fill the hole in his head with a cantaloupe. Then he will remember nothing about Pan."

I groaned. If you want a stupid answer, always ask a Smarty-Pant. "Any other ideas?"

I aLwaYs SUSPECTEd MY TEacHEr was a MELON-hEad.

"You've got worries of your own, young man," Mr. Slomin informed me. "Your social studies project is overdue, and you haven't even chosen a topic yet."

"I have a solution," Stan said sadly. "I, Stan, am the problem. I must not return to Earth."

What? No Stan? My exchange buddy had only been around for three weeks, but he already felt as much a part of the family as Lindsay or Roscoe. Actually, *way* more than Roscoe. "But Earth is the new vacation planet!" I protested. "You have to get ready for all the tourists!"

"The Pan-Pan Travel Bureau will appoint another agent." He lowered his eyes. "I, Stan, have heard that Shakespeare is looking for a new job."

"Shakespeare?!" I almost spat out the name. **"That cheater isn't fit to carry your jock-strap!"**

"Devin," my exchange buddy chided me, "Shkprnys may not be a very honest Pant. But when it comes to the travel business, he has no equal."

"But who'll break all my Rules of Coolness?" I babbled. "Who'll eat our old phone books? Who'll pick his nose in front of everybody at school? Who'll be the biggest dweeb in Clearview?"

"I, Stan, will miss you, too," said my exchange buddy warmly.

"There might be another way," suggested Mark McGwire. "After we drop off Devin, Stan, and Fungus, we can take Mr. Slomin for an extra spin around the sun. This creates a small time warp. That way, Mr. Slomin will arrive on Earth a few minutes *before* he left."

TrYiNg tO uNderstaNd tiME traveL MaKes MY braiN hurt.

"And he won't remember anything," Stan said excitedly, "since it won't have happened yet! That's brilliant!" He turned to the Smarty-Pants. "Can it work?"

Zgrbnys looked disgusted. "Well, I suppose it can. Not as well as replacing his brain with a cantaloupe, of course. But it's worth a try."

By this time, Earth had appeared on the ship's screen, all blue, white, and breathtaking. Pan is okay, I thought to myself, but as planets go, **Earth is a supermodel**.

"You'll never know how close you were to the icebox, old buddy," I told the world.

And then we were going down. I watched the view change: continent, country, state, town, neighborhood, and finally my front yard. Home, sweet home never felt sweeter.

As soon as we stepped off the ship, Fungus beat a hasty retreat to his doghouse. I honestly wished I could have gone with him. I sure wasn't looking forward to explaining all this to my folks.

Then I heard my dad's voice from inside the house. "Why did Devin and Stan just bolt out of here?"

"Because they're crazy?" suggested Roscoe nastily.

The Smarty-Pants were right! The whole trip had taken only a few seconds! We were back at

the night Zgrbnys and Gthrmnys had gone on
Jeopardy! In Earth time, we had just left the room.

I was about to stick the garage-door opener
back in the Honda when I froze. For there, sitting
cross-legged in our driveway, was Mr. Slomin.

"How could he be *here*?" I hissed at Stan. "We
just left him on the ship! He can't be in two
places at once!"

"The time warp!" Stan explained. "Since he went back in time a few extra minutes, he got here *before* us!"

I had to find out for certain. "Mr. Slomin," I asked, "are you okay? Do you remember what happened to you?"

The teacher was dazed and confused. "I'm not sure," he began shakily. "I was on my way to your house, and then—" He shrugged, eyes wide. "The next thing I knew I was here in your driveway." He winced in pain. "With a splitting headache."

"That's a common side effect of time travel," Stan whispered triumphantly.

Mark McGwire's plan had worked! That guy was wasting his time with baseball. He was a *genius*.

Mr. Slomin shook his head. "I have a few other memories, but they don't make any sense—something about underpants—"

"You probably meant to go home and change them," suggested Stan.

Our teacher thought it over.

That's what you get for journeying 85,000 light-years without a change of underwear.

138

"Yes. Yes, of course." His brow knit. "I seem to recall one last thing—an excellent presentation on the achievements of the human race."

I got a great idea. "Oh, that was our social studies project," I told him.

"Right," said Mr. Slomin fuzzily. "It took up your whole garage—"

Three sets of eyes turned to the garage. You could see through the window it was empty.

Mr. Slomin frowned. "What happened to your project?"

"We presented it already." I winked at Stan. "Don't you remember, Mr. Slomin? You gave us an A-plus!"

Someday when I'm ninety, and my best friend, Stan Mflxnys, is 228, I *just might* admit that we didn't really deserve that social studies grade.

But when you think about it, we saved a whole planet. If that isn't worth an A-plus, what is?

Are there really aliens out there?

Are there such things as ghosts?

Is the supernatural really natural?

so weird

The haunting new paperback series that brings the adventures of the supernatural from the TV room to your library.

So Weird #1: Family Reunion
On sale now

Based on the **Live Action Show** on **Disney Channel**

So Weird #2: Shelter
On sale now

So Weird #3: Escape
Coming in May 2000

Disney CHANNEL®

IN BOOKSTORES EVERYWHERE

SoWeird.com